3 *Am Thoughts*

Flairs and Glairs
Publication House

"3 Am Thoughts"

ISBN No: " 978-93-90416-52-3"
1st Edition
Language – English and Hindi

Flairs and Glairs
Publication House
Regd. Under MSME Act.

Disclaimer

This is a work of fiction and solely represent the thoughts of the corresponding authors of the articles. Our editors have tried their best to edit the content of all the authors and check the plagiarism.

All the write-ups in this book are unique and are only published in this book.

In case any plagiarism or error is found, only the author is responsible alone, and not the publisher or the Compilers.

Cover Designing
Shubham Shah

Acknowledgement

First of all we want to thank god almighty who blessed us with the power and zeal to be able to complete this anthology. Also we want to thank our parents who trusted us and let us work at our will. Family support is all that is required to make things easy.

Regarding the anthology we also want to thank all the co-authors o this book who kept their patience and supported us in this journey.

We would also like to extend our gratitude to Shubham shah , the founder of FLAIRS AND GLAIRS and Ishani Agarwal who showed their unconditional support and love to us and who believed that we can do this.

Thanks to one and all.

Co-Author

1. Shubham Shah (Founder Flairs and Glairs)
2. Ishani Agarwal (Co Founder Flairs and Glaies)
3. Aryansh Arora (Compiler)
4. Shiven Gupta (Compiler)
5. Ishika Agarwal
6. Ahshaas Hussain
7. Gaurav Kumar Sharma
8. Lakshita Shrimali
9. Sayali Yelve
10. Dr Rakesh R Mund
11. Sushmitha Vangipuram
12. Lalitha Srinivas
13. Payal Banerjee
14. Rishit Parekh
15. Rahul Raj Tripathi
16. Kirti Goel
17. Shreya Verma
18. Parul Thakur
19. Wilbur Arnold Clarke
20. Chitra Indrajeet Gupta
21. Shreyashi Srivastava
22. Rashika Jain
23. Arushi Chitranshi
24. Anubhuti Sachdeva

25. Naveen Nischal
26. Apoorva Bhardwaj
27. Anubha Gupta
28. Gaurav Nautiyal
29. Tanya Rai
30. Saloni Gupta
31. Mohit Mishra
32. Dhivya Rajamani
33. Shreya Gupta
34. Ayushi Kamble
35. Damini Upadhyay
36. Sakshi Agrawal
37. Chirag L Sagar
38. Sejal Rawat
39. Subhransu Padhy
40. Jeevika Phagwani
41. Alankar Sandeep Maeenkar
42. Bhumika Katyal
43. Gautam Agarwal
44. Sugandha Verma
45. Yash Soni

Shu bham Shah
(Founder- Flairs and Glairs)

Shubham Shah, entrepreneur at "Flairs & Glairs" a brand with dynamics in events organizing and cultural educational pan INDIA, He is a 26yr. old guy who recently has entered, the digital platform of imprinting emotions. He has initiated with his own open mic platform to help budding poets and aspiring writers under his brand named as "Teekhe Zasbaaat" He is a commerce graduate from Bhagalpur City of Bihar.
He says Writing has impersonated him since childhood and he has now been writing for over a decade!

Cooking, on the other hand, is his passion! He also mentions, trying out new things just tickles him!

When asked sir, Why SPICY EMOTIONS?

He smiled and added, "agar jasbaat teekhe na ho toh wo jasbaat kaha" Spices are all that blends! So do his words!

As a chef, he presents to you his dish! Hot and freshly served! Taste it! Feel it! Enjoy it! You can also find his writing in the Solo book "Teekhe Zasbaaat" and 70+ anthologies. With his passion to explore opportunities across Platforms he is working with keen devotion and We wish him all the very best for his future ventures

Share your reviews on his

INSTAGRAM

@spicy_emotions
@shubham4shah

Or via email on

shubham2shah@gmail.com

To stay tuned to his work and opportunities follow his business Handles

INSTAGRAM   FACEBOOK   YOUTUBE

@flairsandglairs
@teekhezasbaaat

WEBSITE:

https://flairsandglairs.in/
https://flairsandglairs.com/

Ishani Agarwal
(Co Founder- Flairs and Glairs)

Born and brought up in Kolkata, she has done her schooling and college from here itself. She is doing her post-graduation at the moment. Ishani loves talking to people around, and is excited for this new beginning of hers! Been a Compiler for 35+

Anthologies, and in the process for more, also, co-authored in 100+ Anthologies, Ishani is very Happy with how her life is turning out now!

Insta handle: Ishani_agarwal_quotes

Aryansh Arora (Compiler)

Aryansh Arora is a dedicated writer from Basti, uttar pradesh who has been featured in 40+ books and he is a guy who is always ready with a perfect work and to face any challenge here. He is 18 years old and he is also author of "KIS KI SUNNE". He has a keen knowledge of poetry writing forms and he is damn impatient. You can see him growing on @shayaryansh it's his instagram account.

Beloved Ones

It was midnight 1:30am and Ryan was on the bed with his diary.He was a bit upset from last 3 weeks and in the end when there was no one to listen what ryan wanted to say,he decided to write it on a paper.We can say.....

A LOVE LETTER!!

Exact at 3am his father came inside the room and found that piece of paper on Ryan's bed .He started reading and within no time he burst into tears.In the end he and his father slept together hugging each other.

The letter was ,

Hey Medhavi !My beautiful lady.I know you love me and I tell you everyday that I love you too.I really miss you dear.I miss you in school,I still remember your cute smile.You are the most beautiful soul I ever saw.I am sorry if I did something wrong.Please come back.I miss you darling!I still love to wear that hoodie you gave me.I even wear it in summers.I don't know where are you right now .These days I am alone,I don't have anyone to share my feelings with.Yesterday teacher taught us that if you want to convey your message to someone who is far away ,you can write a letter.

So I am writing it to you now.Hope you will get this letter soon.I am writing this letter on 3may 2019 .Hope you will get it in a week.I don't know whether you will reply or not but it's okay.

I just want to say I miss you.

I love you medhavi,I love you a lot.

When father saw the name Medhavi he cried like anything because ,
Ryan is a 11 year old boy and this letter is not for his under age girlfriend,it is for her mother.Medhavi is the name of the mother of Ryan who died 3 years ago in a car accident.

MIDNIGHT MEMORIES ARE NOT ALWAYS FOR THE LOVED ONES,SOME TIMES IT IS EVEN FOR THE "BELOVED ONES".

Shiven Gupta (Compiler)

Shiven Gupta is a B.com student from NGPC Lucknow and he belongs to Basti, Uttar Pradesh. He is a passionate badminton and basketball player. Besides , he loves to write what he feels. He is pursuing for CS and he has big dreams in life.

Love

It is not a storybook or a Bollywood movie ,it doesn't come always easy.

Love is overcoming obstacles , facing challenges , fighting to be together but sometimes it's better to just let things be, let people go, don't fight for exposure, don't ask for explanations, don't chase answers and don't expect people to understand. In short word it is easy to spell, difficult to define and hard to live without.

I have spoiled too many unworthy people with my time and attention and make them priorities when they hardly deserved it. It is not worth it when there are people who can hold my hands forever and make efforts for being in it.

Breakup

I think it all started when I stopped liking her, I still loved her but I didn't liked her anymore and that's when I knew my mind is preparing my heart for that moment... the one where would I say " I'm done " and I would really mean that.

Sometimes it is okay to take a step back and admit it is being complicated but that's life I guess it is always complicated the best partner for you at that time is yourself. Do whatever you think is correct and learn to be happy at hard times. Don't let yourself be in pain thinking of things will become simpler , easier and better.

Ishika Agarwal

Ishika is a 16 years old girl.

Writing for her is nothing else but a passion. She hails from the city of Joy and Art. She has been a Co-author in 30+ anthologies in the recent past, all adding on experiences to her.

Been a part of India book of Record projects like Black and World Record projects like 15 wonders of Poetry, Ishika is paving her way to success.

The Moon Sings,

And the stars are the background dancers.
And we all are the audience to all this .
Every night this show takes place.
Some like to see and some don't.
Some wake up till late in the night and some are early sleepers.
A lot of songs are played in a single show every night.
For every single person it conveys a message, which maybe that person needs to hear.
For me, it helps me express my thoughts and help me write.
I love to write at night and some of my best works are night written.
The moon not just sings but listen too.
He acts like a therapist for me.
It gives me solutions and support that I need.
I need to thank you for being there in my dark times when no one was there but you.

Ahshaas Hussain

Ahshaas Hussain, an M.A. English student in Gangadhar Meher University, Sambalpur. He is a Gold Medalist in English Honors (B.A.), Kathak Dancer, a National Level Swimmer, Classical Singer, a Survivor and a Teacher. He has completed his Diploma in Arts and crafts from Lalit Kala Academy, Bhubaneswar. He is an ardent lover of English Literature, Nature and Animals. Once, a kid asked him, whether he believes in magic or not. He answered, "I believe that every person has magic in them. It's up to them how much of fairy dust they sprinkle on every person they meet". He is the co-author of 80+ Anthologies and the compiler of 10+ anthologies. He strongly believes in the motto, "Bloom for Yourself."

Life Is Beautiful

Somedays it feels like
I'm being injected with needle
Carrying the dose of happiness
Pricking my mind
Those chills moving
Through my spine
A capillary action
From my legs till my heart
Making it jump with life
I know it won't last long
Like all my friendships
That fade under sand of time
So all I do say
"I love you" a little more
To the ones who see my sadness
More than the bright days
I try to gift my smiles
Giggles and laughters to my mother
A supporting hand to my father
Those bubbly fights to my sister
Till this high remains
For I know the moment it dies
I collapse back again
Sleeping under the
Blanket of numbness
Eating away air
To give my body a
Taste of freedom
In the hope

My inside won't feel trapped anymore
The moment of ecstacy
When strikes
I make sure to listen
To those shallow words, "Be Happy" they say
Once in a while
As rare or as frequent it happens
I tell my mind
"After all life is not that bad
Perhaps life is afterall beautiful.

Gaurav Kumar Sharma

Gaurav Kumar Sharma is an Electrical Engineer and Teacher too. He was born and raised in Chapra, Bihar. He has the hobbies of photography, graphics designing & poetry. Although he is not a professional writer but he love to write. Having such varied interest makes person to explore and give rise to sense of uniqueness into them. You can follow him on Instagram page @shutterpedia7.

एक एहसास

परिंदो को संभाला है आसमानों ने,
सूरज की रौशनी भी डूब जाती है सागर की बाँहो में,
जब ठंडी हवा के झोंके
सागर की लहरो से टकराती है,
जैसे मानो तेरे होने का एहसास दे जाती है ।
तारों की टीम टिमाहट के बीच
जब चाँद की रौशनी नजर आती है,
सागर की लहरे भी बोल जाती है
वाह! क्या खूब बनाया है कुदरत ने,
मानो जैसे चाँदनी रात मे
सागर मे जलपरी नजर आती है।
खुदा ने भी तरासा होगा तेरे लिए सागर से भी गहरा दिल,
जैसे शांत सागर को भी हल्की हवा महसूस हो जाती है,
सागर की लहरे जब खामोश हो जाती है
मानो जैसे तेरी खामोशी
मुझे दर्द दे जाती है ।

सफ़र- ए- ज़िंदगी

सोच कर कभी हैरान मत होना जिंदगी मे,
क्या खोया, क्या पाया जिंदगी मे,
हैरान वो होते है,
जो कुछ न कर पाते है जिंदगी मे ।

मुश्क़िले तो हर रास्ते मे आती है
नदी का पानी भी बीच पथरो से टकराती है,
परेशान मत होना उन पथरो से,
ये वही पथर है,
जो हमारी मंजिलो का रास्ता बनाती है ।

Lakshita Shrimali

Lakshita Shrimali is a student at Banasthali Vidyapith. She wrote this when she was in 12th grade. She is passionate about writing. She aims to be a famous author after she grows up. She is looking forward to excel in the field of commerce with working on her passion for writing. She is also the author of 'IT'S UNPREDICTABLE'.
Instagram Handle- @lakshitashrimali.\

Fairytail

There was a princess,
A separated one from town.
She was not pretty,
But she had a heart divine.
She was crazy,
About a prince smart and flawless of that time.
Princess was afraid of rejections,
That's why she never confessed her feelings because
her mind denied.
With a smile at her face she accepted the reality,
She didn't deserve him because she wasn't perfect
in the community
Prince was amazing inside out,
She always admired him and daily wrote him a note.
A witch entered in the life of the prince,
The witch took capture him all.
The princess started talking to the prince
And being fascinated towards the princess the prince
even felt in love.
The witch was eliminated despite of being gorgeous,
The princess won without any rejections.
Prince and Princess lived happily ever after
Desperate in love they were meant to be forever.

Us

Sometimes when I feel separated from world,
I sit to write.
With millions of thoughts in my mind,
Only you are the one about whom I rhyme.
Thoughts of us revolve around every time.
That struggle to escape and those amazing rides.
That sunset and those roads,
That jacket and never ending talks.
Those movies and that fun,
That park and us.
That football and badminton,
That coaching and each and every bunk.
Daily trip to temple,
And those giggles of ours.
Going to temptations and having lots of fun,
These Memories won't fade till eternity and there is
no escape from these and no run.
I wish could relive it all,
When we were so obsessed over each other.
I wish could again read that journal,
Sitting outside the park together.

Sayali Yelve

Hailing from Mira Road, Thane, and beauty of hometown Ratnagiri, Maharashtra. A budding prolific writer, well versed and known for her works in English, Hindi, and Marathi. Graduated in Computer programming, she is technically sound and uses that to her corporate in her words. Now being an Entrepreneur and a Teacher she is vivid and creative in her imagination and intense passion for writing has enabled Miss. Sayali to reach the hearts of the readers, by the use of beautifully sculpted words.You can see her works on YouTube, WordPress, and Insta as well. Insta Id: thoughts_that_make_life.

<u>मंज़िल</u>

अक्सर अजनबी उस राह मिलते है,
जहा की मंज़िल काफी सख्त होती है,
आफ़ताब की आब भी,
घेर ले ऐसी वो मुलाकात होती है ||
टकरा गए हो मानो दो दिल,
उस अनजान रास्तें पर,
ढूंढ रहे हो खुदको,
एक दूसरे के आलम के तख्त पर ||
कुछ अल्फ़ाज़ होते है,
तो कही सरगम जाग उठते है,
किसीकी फरमाइश मे,
तो आलाप भी गहराई से लिए जाते है ||
इसे इश्क तो ना कह सकेंगे,
ये तो बस शरुवात है,
कुछ अच्छे किस्से बुनने की बात है,
शायद ये आने वाले उन प्यारे लम्हों की आहट है... !

At The Stroke Of 3!

I happened to wake up, at the stroke of 3,
Felt as if the night was calling me,
On that cozy bed when I fell asleep,
The stars twinkled forever thee...

I saw him sit right next to me,
Working was he,
His hands over me,
And me smiling looking at him...

But the breeze blew harsh,
I happened to cling him agast,
To the thunders,
I woke up now...

I fetched him all over,
Couldn't see him anyhow,
Was it a dream, I dreamt somehow,
And I'm still wandering searching for him now!

Dr Rakesh R Mund

Dr Rakesh R Mund has been participating in more than 70 anthology and his solo book ishq-e-panhi available on amazon and flifpkart. He read veda and diffrent literatures which give a glimpse on his writing. You can contact with him : insta-Rakeshmundr_.

तुटा ख़्वाब

ख़्वाब तुटा रात थी गहरी
प्रारंभ नयी कहानि,
न मिला कूछ ख़ास वही
वो उजरत पूरानी,
एक चेहरा जो इंधन है
जीवन के सफ़र में,
होती है ऐसी परिस्थिति
तुम हो नौ-सफ़र में ।
घूम रहा इश्क़ के फिराक में
होके मैं बेहाल,
नहीं है तुमसे न मिलने का
दिल में मलाल,
सोचता रहता हूँ सिर्फ एक
पल ही मिले ,
बता सकूँ अपने आशिकी के
अश्क ही खिले ।
हम-नफ़स मेरे मान भी जा तु
मेरे इबादत को समझ,
कितने कितने आशिक हो चुके
ध्वस्त सहादत को समझ,
असरार है मोहब्बत में थोड़ी
हिम्मत चाहिए,
खुल जाएगा वो रहस्य तेरी
सहमत चाहिए ।
बे-लौस चाहत है तु तेरे लिए
जीवन के पतंग भी कटे,

तेरे खूशी के लिए तयार हूँ
कहे तो सतरंज भी बटे ,
झुका नहीं आजतक सामने
कौई तूफान भी हो,
मंजूरी है तु कहे तो हर्ष के साथ
झुकूं मेहमान भी हो ।

Sushmitha Vangipuram

Sushmitha is an educator by profession. She comes from Andhra Pradesh.She lives in Surat. She is passionate about writing. She writes quotes, musings, stories and poems. Her writings mainly include nature.She is also passionate about astronomy.She participates in writing competitions online. Besides writing, she is also interested in gardening.

True Love

After a splendid dinner, Abhiram sat on his chair in the verandah.He was amused to see full moon through the leaves of trees which were dancing to the cool breeze coming from far away mountains that night.He got lost into thoughts of lady he admired,Geetha.She was most renowned poet of her times.Abhiram never missed to read her poems in his busy schedule.

Though they did not see each other , letters exchanged their talks,opinions and much more.

One day he wrote a letter to her expressing his admiration and affection towards her.Surprisingly,she accepted his proposal.His happiness knew no bounds.They decided to meet at her house. He was anxious to see her. Finally, the day arrived.He went to her house.He was made to sit in hall by maid.Geetha came to him. She was draped in a beautiful saree.She looked like an angel.She introduced him to her parents.The only barrier to their love was the fact that he was an orphan.

Meanwhile,a very familiar hand on his shoulders woke him up from his thoughts.That was his wife Geetha,smiling at him,holding their grand daughter in her arms. They played with their grand daughter for some time and made her sleep.

Lalitha Srinivas

Lalitha Srinivas , lives in Andhra Pradesh who graduated with computer science engineering. Been part of many anthologies as a co-author. Being a home maker, she creates a beautiful art either it's with ink filled in pen on a paper or brush dipped in paint on a canvas. She is a traveller who wish to explore the beauty of INDIA, it's different cultures and different cuisines. She started writing and handling her page at Instagram just to dedicate it to her late friend who committed suicide. And wanted no one to take such decisions she wished to interact with people to inspire them and understand their pain. Whenever you feel alone, ping on..
Insta I'd: @celebrate_golden_days.

Incomplete

Light walks into my life, like a moon in the sky.
Not ful fledged.
One day, it brightens
the world.
One day, it darkens
the world.
Sometimes it's too early.
Sometimes it's too late.
But it's the life cycle.
Just like our Happiness and sadness.
Sometimes they complete our life.
Sometimes they remains incomplete.

Long Distance Relationship

I still remember the mornings,
when you and me wake up too early.
You lie to do gym, I lie to do meditation.
We both used to step on terrace.
By settling a side, picking up our phones.
With the early morning sunrise,
You and me having a bright smile.
Looking at each other and
Laughing at our silly lies.
Just to call each other to increase,
The love of our long distance relationship.

Payal Banerjee

Proudest Writer From Kolkata.
 Happiest Co-Author Pursuing English Honours.
Girl, with wings flying high creating Rainbow of her own.

छोटा सा गाँव

मेरा दिल एक छोटा सा गांव हैं
गिनती के कुछ लोग ही है यहाँ ,
रोशनी भी नहीं हैं, ना ही बिजली हैं.

लेकिन जब तुम मिलने आए,
बरसों की रात में भी ,
सूरज की सुबह जैसी रोशनी खिल आई.
सब कुछ सुबह सा साफ़ दिखने लगा .
इतना साफ़ की तुम्हारे दिल मे घर किए ,
शक़ को भी मैंने देख लिया .
बिल्कुल मैं उसी शक़ की बात कर रही हूँ
जिसने मेरे प्यार को इज़्ज़त से कलंक तक का सफर करा दिया.
जिसने तुम्हें मुझे अपनाने से इंकार,
और साथ मे माँगी दुआओं को बेकार करार कर दिया .
शक़ देखकर मैंने रास्ता तो बदल दिया ,
लेकिन दिल को कैसे बदलूँ ?
दर्द को मुस्कान की चादर से तो ढक दिया
मन मे लिखे नाम को कैसे भूलूं?

अजीब सा प्यार

अजीब सा प्यार था हमारा
एक दूसरे को ही डाटते
एक दूसरे की ही परवा करते
एक दूसरे पे ही गुस्सा करते
एक दूसरे को ही प्यार करते
साथ मे हस्ते साथ मे रोते
सब कुछ करते
लेकिन एक दूसरे के बिना एक पल नहीं ग्वारा
गुस्से मे ही सही एक दूसरे की आवाज सुन कर सुकून मिलता
नाराज ही सही एक दूसरे को देखकर दिल को करार मिलता
आज अलग होकर भी हमे सुकून है
 बात करने की परवा नहीं
एक दूसरे का खयाल नहीं
दूर होकर भी हम पास है
अधूरे होकर भी आज हम पूरे है
आज मंजिले भी अलग है
और हाथ थामे ख्वाहिशें भी
किसी मोड़ पे फिर मिलकर
बिछड़ने की आश हैं.
उन्हीं यादों के साथ,
आगे बढ़ने की ये प्यास हैं.
तुम और मैं होकर भी आज हम 'हम' है,
क्या सच मे इतना अजीब था हमारा प्यार !

Rishit Parekh

Most of the writers start writing after going through breakups or a hard phase. But Rishit has altogether a different story. It is his girls charm & beauty that makes him capture all her innocence in a diary & present it to the world. Most of his write-ups revolve around his girl. By profession he is a teacher, so you can address him as, "A teacher by profession and a poet by heart."

क्या है वह जो तुझे सताता है

क्या है वह जो तुझे सताता है,
क्यों नहीं तू भी आसमान की तरफ अपना सर उठाता है,
क्यों नहीं लोगों को अपनी तकलीफ तू बताता है,
क्या है वह जो तुझे सताता है...
किस बात का तुझे दर है,
एक तू है और मिलों तक फैला यह अंबर है,
हिम्मत तो कर, उड़ने को तेरे पास भी पर है,
फिर भला किस बात का तुझे दर है...
तुझे किस बात की अब राह है,
हासिल कर जो भी तेरी चाह है,
हर कदम पर अल्लाह की तुझपर निगाह है,
तो फिर किस बात की तुझे अब राह है...
मुस्कुरा थोड़ा के पास अब किनारा है,
दुखों का हट चुका कोहरा है,
खुल चुका खुशियों का पतारा है,
की अब तो थोड़ा मुस्कुरा और देख कितना पास तेरे
किनारा है...

वे मुस्कराते फूल नहीं

वे मुस्कराते फूल नहीं
जिनको आता है मुरझाना
वे तारों के दीप नहीं
जिनको भाता है बुझ जाना...

वे न हारे थे न अब हारे है,
वे तो शून्य पर सवार है,
शोर भरी इस दुनिया में,
वे अपने आप में एक सुकून है...

था वीराना सा जीवन पहले उनका,
मगर अब यह मंज़र वे बदलेंगे,
उनके अंदर छिपे जुनून से वे,
आसमान से भी ऊपर तक जाएंगे...

है जो फितूर कामयाबी का सवार उनके सर पर,
तो अब वे कामयाब होके ही दम लेंगे,
नज़र लोगों की होगी ऊँची जब देख उन्हें,
तब उनके भी दिल खुलके मुस्कुराएंगे...

Rahul Raj Tripathi

A textrovert.
Music is my drug.
 Engineer in making.
Instagram-leo_a_textrovert

जब मैं मर जाऊं

जब मैं मर जाऊं सफेद लिबास में आना तुम
कफ़न से नहीं मेरी कविताओं से सजा देना
उस बेजान बस्ती में जाना तुम
धीरे से एक कहकहा लगा देना।

जब मैं मर जाऊं हटाना मेरा तकिया
उस तस्वीर को गुलाबों से सजा देना
मेरे नाम को कोसने से पहले
उस तकिए को गले से लगा लेना।

जब मैं मर जाऊं ज़माने से नज़ारे मिलाना
एक दीवाना था सबको बता देना
किसी दूसरे से रिश्ते निभाने से पहले
गिले शिकवे सभी मिटा लेना।

जब मैं मर जाऊं महकते पत्रों को जलाने से पहले
मेरी मां को दिखा देना
गुनाहों की संख्या गिनाने से पहले
अपनी लिखावट मिटा देना।

जब मैं मर जाऊं उदास मत होना दावत बुला लेना
कोई दिखे मेरे जैसा उससे दूरियां बना लेना
शरीख नहीं हो पाऊंगा तो क्या
मेरी जगह मेरे यार बुला लेना।

जब मैं मर जाऊं गुस्साना नहीं मेरी यादों पे
नादानियों का नाम लगा देना
तेरा गुस्सा भी तो बड़ा प्यारा है

गुस्से से नफ़रत मत बढ़ा लेना।
जब मैं मर जाऊं अश्कों की इजाज़त ले लेना
मेरी अस्थियां भीगा देना
पावन हाथों से अपने
किसी दरिया में बहा देना।

Shayari

खुशी से बांट दी सब खुशियां मेरे हिस्से की
बटोरोगे इन्हें तो ज़माना मिलेगा
कुछ शब्द तोड़ कर बिखेरे हैं मेरी कविताओं में
समेटोगे इन्हें तो नाम तुम्हारा मिलेगा।

Kirti Goel

A medical professional soaked in the love of poetry. She believes everyone has something special that needs to be explored. She explored her inner self & got gifted by the galaxy of words inside her.

Through her nib, she inks the reality of life and expresses her true self. She believe all we need is a heart to write & words to express. You can reach out to her musings on instagram @poetryy_fair

For her readers, she wanted to say :

"Their is always a story to begin"

So, buckle up your laces and write your Life Story Yourself

सोचती हूं

सोचती हूं
छोड़ कर सब कुछ
निकल पड़ूं ...

निकल पड़ूं... जहां खुली हवाएं हों
सीधे साधे लोगों का साथ हो
जहां हवाओं में बहता कोई राग हो
पानी में जहां दिलों सी मिठास हो

सोचती हूं
छोड़ कर सब कुछ
निकल पड़ूं !!

निकल पड़ूं... जहां घर पहुंचने की जल्दी ना हो
जहां बाट तुम्हारी कोई तकता ना हो
जहां दूर दूर तक कोई छोर ना हो
सरपट दौड़ती जिंदगी का शोर ना हो

सोचती हूं
छोड़ कर सब कुछ
निकल पड़ूं....

निकल पड़ूं... जहां नफरतों की दीवार ना हो
झूठे दिखावे का कोई द्वार ना हो

जहां मन में कोई शंका ना हो
गिद्धों सी छुपी कोई मंशा ना हो

सोचती हूं
छोड़ कर सब कुछ
निकल पड़ूं
अपनी ही रेची दुनिया में
जहां पल पल बदलते रंग तो हो
पर रंग बदलते लोग ना हो
सोचती हूं निकल पड़ूं
ऐसी ही किसी दुनियाँ में !!

Shreya Verma

I am Shreya Verma from a small city in Uttar Pradesh (Basti).. Professionally want to be a lawyer but writing is passion.. I write what i feel mainly my surroundings and imagination give me a wing to create a content.. Not a extraordinary writer but a small contribution to this poetry world..

"कुछ राते बिताई थी अकेले,
तभी तो लिखना जाना था,
उतारते गई एक - एक लफ्ज़ यू पन्नों पे,
उस दिन शायद स्याही को अपना मना था।"

"कुछ राते बिताई थी अकेले,

पहला कदम

बंद कमरे में एक लड़की अनजानी सी,
खुद को अब वो ना मानती रूहानी सी,
रहती थी वो अकेले अंधेरी दीवारों में,
और कुछ बदलाव था आजकल उसके व्यव्हारो में।
हर रात वो खुद को खुद में कहीं खोजती थी,
गुनाह हुआ है उससे शायद यही सोचती थी,
जाने कितना दोषी वो खुद को मानने लगी,
दूसरो के नज़रिए से ही खुद को जानने लगी।
पहले जो घंटो हँसती थी,
आज वो कहीं खो गई,
शायद उन दरिंदो की वजह से,
अब वो खुद के लिए सो गई।

चार लोग की बाते,
उसके मन में चुभने लगी है,
बिना गलती के भी खुद को,
अब वह दोषी समझने लगी है।
एक हादसे ने मानो उसे वीरान कर दिया,
और गूँजती बातो ने जीना उसका हराम कर दिया।
उसके जिस्म को हेवानो ने नोचा था,
उसके रूह को भी हर हद तक खरोचा था।
ये सब अब उससे ना सहा जा रहा था,
बंद कमरों में अब ना रहा जा रहा था,

जाने कितने लोग उसे रोक रहे थे,
घर में बंद रहने के लिए टोक रहे थे।
सबकी बातो को अनसुना कर,
वो खुद को इंसाफ दिलाने जा रही थी,
और घर से बाहर " पहला कदम " खुद के लिए आज बढ़ा
रही थी।

Parul Thakur

Parul Thakur writes about the various emotions that you encounter and fail to explain. She is an 18 year old author from Delhi, India. Her educational background is in journalism and mass communication (Currently pursuing) from Noida. Apart from writing, she loves birds and cooking. For more updates you can follow her on her instagram handle @_paperboats.16 . You can also check out her write-ups on https://paperboat-16.blogspot.com.

Romance Of Existence

It's been a year.
Dried up all my tears.
I have been living in my own corpse.
Few days back, some new friends of mine,
Were identified living in me back then.
It's a misery to not sing at all,
And to go silent all through those days.
They all are great friend,
But I don't want to live with them.
I remember the day they were identified,
I learned to live,
I learned to respect my existence.
But they are a curse.
I am told to maintain a distance,
But I feel its against my existence.
During those intrinsic days,
I have fallen in the clutch of circumstances,
Hiding all my pain,
And beyond these looms, wrath, tears.
And those starry night, horror shade and heavenly jumps.
In the menance of years,
You will find me unafraid.
No matter how much pain and punishment,
I might go through.
I will transmute,
I am the mistress of my fate.
I am the captain of my soul,

I will win this battle all on my own.
I will kill my pain and overcome it,
As if I am insane.

Wilbur Arnold Clarke

Wilbur Arnold Clarke an aspiring 20 years old poet/actor/sketch artist was born and brought up in Faridabad, Haryana. He is currently pursuing Journalism from Lingaya's Lalita Devi Institute of Management and Sciences, Chattarpur, New Delhi. These are his first poems which have been published. You can check out other poems by Wilbur on https://ehsaas06.blogspot.com and follow him on his instagram handle (@w.arnoldclarke6700) for more work. You can also mail him at tomclarke.cruise@gmail.com.

Broken Wings

Today's whites are turning black,
Tomorrow's blacks will be ashes.
All good things have gone today,
I want to go back to yesterday.

Life becoming a complex puzzle,
What does it mean? All I ask...
Surrounded by snakes of a thousand questions,
Seeing the future, the hidden past
The foundations shaken to shatter.
All I want is to fly.
With my broken wings,
Seeing the future, past left behind.

Danger fought with anger,
Calcite like hands, gloom forefront.
Let me face the storm and not return.
The misery of time turning me numb.

Who is to blame? I wonder...
Is it a mistake?
No matter how much I refuse to cry,
Seeing the future, the hidden past
The foundations shaken to shatter.
All I want is to fly.
With my broken wings,
Seeing the future, past left behind.

Secret

A secret I don't wish to withhold
With a hope it might make you smile
To tell you, I must muster courage
It will take a while
I know we are just friends
But I want something more
To call you my love
Whom my heart adores

Chitra Indrajeet Gupta

I am chitra indrajeet gupta and i basically belong to Gujarat and after marriage I live in basti, uttar Pradesh. My Hobbies are writing books,painting,dancing etc. It is only because of my husband that I am still alive and happy and passionate about my hobbies.
EMAIL-poojaindrajeetgupta@gmail.com

तेरी मेरी कहानी

मैंने जब उसे पहली बार देखा तो लगा जैसे हवाएं चलने लगी मधुर संगीत बजने लगा दिल मेरा जोर से धड़कने लगा फिर अचानक सब रुकता गया उसने मुझे पलट कर देखा फिर वह आगे चला गया अगली बार वह मुझे एक शादी में मिला वहां पर उसने मुझे देखा मेरी वही हालत थी जो पहले थी पता है मुझे यह फिल्मी बातों की तरह है लेकिन सच में मेरे साथ ऐसा ही हुआ वह मुझे अपने दोस्त से मिलाना चाहता था पर मैं तो उसी के ख्यालों में खोई थी हमारी दोस्ती उसी शादी से शुरू हुई वह मुझे अपनी दोस्त की प्रेमिका बनाना चाहता था पर मैं तो इसी बहाने उसके दोस्त बने रहना चाहती थी धीरे-धीरे हमारी दोस्ती आगे बढ़ी फिर एक दिन अचानक हमारी लड़ाई हो गई उसकी वजह उनका मित्र था कुछ दिन तक बोलचाल बंद हो गया फिर अचानक हमारी मुलाकात हुई लेकिन हम लोग एक दूसरे को रोक नहीं पाए बात करने से दोस्ती गहरी होती गई मैं तो उनसे शुरू से ही प्यार करती थी पर उन्हें इस बात का एहसास नहीं था एक दिन मैंने उनसे अपने दिल की बात कह दी शुरू शुरू में वह नाराज थे कुछ दिन तक उन्होंने मेरा जवाब नहीं दिया एक दिन उन्होंने मुझे फोन किया उस दिन ऐसा लग रहा था जैसे कोई सर पर बंदूक रखा हो हम दोनों की आवाजें ही नहीं निकल रही थी हम दोनों ही डरे हुए थे उन्होंने कहा कि वह भी मेरे बिना नहीं रह सकती उन्हें भी नींद नहीं आ

रही कुछ भी अच्छा नहीं लग रहा है हम दोनों ही बहुत खुश थे लेकिन साथ में डर इस बात का था कि हमारे प्यार का अंजाम क्या होगा तुमसे कब वह आप बन गए इस बात का मुझे पता ही नहीं चला हमारी दोस्ती प्यार में बदल गई थी सब अच्छा जा रहा था हम लोग बहुत खुश थे 1 दिन घर पर सब को पता चल गया सब हम दोनों से बहुत नाराज थे शुरू में हम लोग को बहुत डर था कि कहीं हमारी कहानी यहीं तक तो नहीं थी लेकिन हमने हार नहीं मानी सारी परिस्थितियों का सामना किया और अंत में हम जीत गए सबने हमारे प्यार को स्वीकार कर लिया और हमारी शादी करवा दी शादी के 1 साल बाद हमारा बेटा दिलजीत हुआ जिसने हमारी पूरी जिंदगी बदल दी और कुछ दिनों बाद अर्जित हुआ जिसके आने से सारी कमी पूरी हो गई अब हम सब एक साथ बहुत खुश है सब भगवान की कृपा है आशा है मेरी कहानी आप सबको पसंद आएगी मैं बस यह कहना चाहती हूं कि जिंदगी में तो उतार-चढ़ाव आते ही रहते हैं पर हमें कभी हार नहीं मानी चाहिए और हर परेशानी का डटकर सामना करना चाहिए|

Shreyashi Srivastava

Shreyashi Srivastava is pursuing engineering from MMIT siddharthanagar . She started writing since 8th standard . Apart from writing ,she is a host of horn ok please. According to her the writings are not just the collection of words but they are the feelings which she loves to Express in the form of words.

अल्फाज अभी है नहीं

कहने को और सुनने को अल्फाज अभी है नहीं ,
एक चीख सी है कानों में मगर चीखें तो हम है नहीं,
है सब हकीकत यहां यह है सब रियाकारी ,
और अगर सब है हकीकत तो फिर कैसी बेकरारी,
कार्निस पर सजे खिताब अब मुझे चुभने लगे हैं ,
हम अपने ही हुनर से छुपने लगे हैं,
बदलते वक्त की बड़ी सटीक सी आवाज़ है ,
खुशी और गम करारा जवाब है,
यही हंसाती है और यही आंखें नम कर देती है,
यह जिंदगी है ए रफीक!! हर पन्ने पर नई कहानी लिख देती है।

पिंजरा

खोल दो यह पिंजरा मुझे आसमान से चाहत है,
आखिर आजादी से तो सबको मोहब्बत है,
मेरे आंसू थमने दो एक मौका दे दो इन आंखों को,
पर अनदेखा कर दिया तुमने मेरे ख्वाबों को,
कोरे थे कागज पर मेरे थे जब चाहती उनमें रंग भर देती,
मैं अपने सारे ख्वाब पूरे कर लेती,
लड़की हूं पर मेरा मकसद सिर्फ घर संभालना नहीं है,
अब बस बहुत हुआ मुझे रोके इतना काबिल यह जमाना नहीं है,
अपने हौसले से मैं सारे ख्वाब अब पूरे करूंगी,
जख्मी हो जाए भले मेरे हाथ पर मैं यह पिंजरा तोड़ के रहूंगी।

Rashika Jain

Rashika jain is a beginner from jaora, madhya pradesh she is 17 years old. She is in 12th grade right now. Writing is her passion. She is looking forward to excel in the field of commerce with working on her passion for writing.
@ink.it_link.it
@gold._grace.27.

All I Want Is You

All i want is to meet you , holding your hands and walk miles,
Our mouth will be shut, but will talk through eyes.
Knowing and choosing you was the best decision of my life,
All i want is to be yours as your wife.
Sometimes i feel scared about us about our future,
But then i feel that you will definitely win my dad's heart by your nature.
Having you as my soulmate, my better half is such a blessing for me,
Promise me that you will make you and me , we.
Imagining my life without you, bring tears in my eye,
But i know you won't leave me and will always be my smile.
Now, come baby lets pray to our god for keeping us together forever,
And i will prove you what, forever means by being with you forever and ever.

Hostel

Going to hostel from home is the worst,
but being in hostel with the funniest roomies is the best.
On the next morning, some were with the buckets and some with tooth brush,
standing in a line, waiting for their turn. And time runs
Like hell. First day of new school for us was like this world for the new born child,
some teachers were cute some were nice but the oldies were so riled.
Daring was bunking the lectures with the besties,
then walking on the street or eating in the canteens.
Everyone was eagerly waiting for the weekend holiday,
So that one can sleep as much as they want as they can't do it everyday.
Now the hostel mates become a second family,
Every one could understand or handle each other very nicely.
"Those were the golden days with happiness and pain,
I wish i could live those golden days again."

Arushi Chitranshi

Arushi Chitranshi, is a business student by day and a poet by night.Dabbling into everything creative, poetry has always been her first love.When she's not writing verses on a paper, she's working in media and content. She started this journey of weaving words into stories from 5th grade. And this has been a long journey to discovery of love and meaning of loss. Turning this turmoil into poetry has been her life's aim.

Someday

I'd like to believe I told you.
Maybe not in words, though.
But, I always told you.
That someday if I knew you enough,
I will get tired of picking your brain
And finding thoughts of someone else running
through it.
Worse even, looking in your heart
And having to find someone else there.
 I think I had warned you a Long time ago
That someday this will happen.
With half-hearted texts and insults hidden under
smiles.
Questioning your ill-placed trust with
every secret you'd reveal to me.
I had told you that it's of no use;
That the consequences will not
justify the good that came out of it;
That I had not built these walls in a day,
Nor without a reason.
They were built to enclose a lifetime of pain,
Emotions I wasn't allowed to feel,
And losses you wouldn't wish upon your worst
enemy.

But you didn't get it then, did you?
What you were signing up for
when you signed up for this.
 I told you then,
That Someday it will not be funny, anymore.
Because your words will have value -
Words to which my heart will respond in ways
I haven't ever fathomed. You see?
I told you in a thousand little ways that I knew how
To try not to fix me with words and thoughts,
And I think you knew.
You have known it all along.
But, you told me not to think too much,
to not read too deeply into it.
It may have worked, I think, this little advice of
yours,
Had you only told me not to Feel at all.

See, I told you someday this would happen
It happens to the best of us, doesn't it?
And I am only Human.
Someday, when you are walking next to me,
Telling me little things you liked about this girl,
you met through a friend of yours.
I will feel like the world around me is collapsing;
Eyes welled up, heart sunk to despair,

And fake smiles will not be enough to cover them
up.
 And Maybe, just maybe, if I took a step back,
It will be like this whole thing never happened.
Maybe someday when I've forgotten all about this
it will be like waking up from a bad dream.
And I hope someday when I'm at my lowest,
I will not feel the urge to call you at 3 AM
just because you'll know what to say.
Someday, maybe
just not Today.

Anubhuti Sachdeva

Anubhuti sachdeva is a writer by hobby from Basti,uttar pradesh.She wants to be a dietitian and have a dream of opening a NGO.
Completed class 12 and now is ready to take flight in new world of Banasthali.

Love At The Ends Of Highways

The hitch between us
are long running highways.
I wish,I could be a swallow,
reaching you by flyways.
Even you are far aways.
My heart gives a beat in your ways .
A day without you is hard to pass .
I don't know how long this will last .
The only door which connects us is love .
In shades,in rains,in sun's gaze,
the only thought in my head is you .
My life is insignificant without you .
When I breathe,I can feel you
and each of it says ...
I LOVE YOU.

हमारा प्यार

दूरी है हमारे बीच
कुछ ज्यादा सी।
खुदा से है दरख़ास्त
एक छोटी सी••
हमारा प्यार हो जैसे बेतोड़ तार।
मिलते हो जब चार यार,
कहे की प्यार हो तो इस प्रकार।
अन्बन चाहे हो दो-चार,
प्यार हमारा रहे सदा बरकरार।
हो हर तरफ प्यार का ही इकरार।
जिन्दगी बन जाये सुन्दर फंकार
बजती रहे यू ही मीठी झंकार।
जब हो हम साथ ,
खुशिओं से भर जाये पूरा संसार ।

Naveen Nischal

Naveen Nischal a budding Poet who is 20 years old and who holds a good command in singing as well was born and brought up in Ghaziabad, Uttar Pradesh. He is currently pursuing a Bachelor of Arts in Journalism & Mass Communication (BA-JMC) from New Delhi. "हक़ीक़त - ए - हयत" is his first poem which has been published. You can follow him on Instagram as @_naveennischal_
You can also mail him at
naveennischal@gmail.com.

हक़ीक़त - ए – हयत

ये हक़ीक़त - ए - हयत,
कुछ बयां करती हैं

स्याहीं भरी दुनियां में,
उस आफ़ताब सा चमकना सिखाती हैं

ये फरेब नहीं मगर,
इसकी भी एक फरेबी हैं

कभी सेहर सी रौशन,
कभी शाम सी ये ढलती हैं

इसकी इनायतो में,
इसकी रंजिशें हैं

जन्म देती मगर,
फिर मौत की आगोश में समा लेती हैं

ये हक़ीक़त - ए - हयत,
कुछ बयां करती हैं

दुनियां हसीन कर,
इश्क़ भी सिखलाती हैं

इस हयत की हैं ये रिवायत,
जिसे ये उल्फत का नाम दे जाती हैं

हैं ये एक खुशनुमा सा एहसास,
जिसकी कुर्बतों में हमें फ़ना कर जाती हैं

इसकी ही तो हैं ये जादूगरीं,
जो इस स्याहीं सी दुनियां को भी हसीन कर देती हैं

चाहत की इस राह पर,
मुसलसल हमारी आष्ना की तलाश करवाती हैं

ये हक़ीक़त - ए - हयत,
ख़ामोशी में,
यूंही गुम हो,
कुछ बयां करती हैं|

Apoorva Bhardwaj

Hey,

This is Apoorva Bhardwaj

I'm from Kolkata, staying in Bangalore and working with Amazon since 3 years, an Engineer, a passionate dancer.

I've started writing since my high school due to a lot of reasons, one out of which was, expressing.

I couldn't draw out my emotions, and then succumbed myself for not being able to be expressive.

Thank you for the opportunity.

I Miss You

But deep down you miss him
Don't you?
Everything peaceful,
with the hunch of rendezvous,
I do check our picturesque!

And the relation with deep hue.
Meaning wouldn't be understood
Loving you couldn't be stopped
Like a lock to my keys,
He had my eyes laid onto,
Like the savour I had his chain,
I guess love was locked in strain.

I knew he could love me but,
He was lost on his road,
He was helpless to leave but,
He was happy and relieved.

I'm still writing and you're still weaving,
You're thanking of the separation,
You're still the better one!

Cuz you evolved,completely!

Plethora

From being in my notes
To being in my dreams
From loving you so much
To hating you beneath,
From concealing feelings with stone
To never see your face or meet a soul
I've learnt it all
The fear I've overcome
The joy, the happiness, the contentment
I feel it all again
To the phoenix of the very own, Roar
To the wings spreading from the castle
Hush hush baby girl, you're the hustle.
You talk about soul!
I talk about persistence,
You talk about confide?
I've always been the one to hide!
Never again shall I abide,
Your rules, aah, Shun the norms of life!

Anubha Gupta

My name is Anubha Gupta
I am 19 years old
I have studied from st. Basil's school
I have dropped 1 year for the preparation of NIFT from lucknow .My desire is to be a successful fashion designer
I have prepared for NIFT exam from pahal lucknow
 I am going to private college for my further studies in my own field My hobbies are sketching , stiching , painting ,dancing and singing My insta handle is anubhagupta0520
And I also have a page on insta where i post my sketches
So my another insta handle is vision_thread05
I am a person full of dreams I am an introvert
I Do like making new friends
I work hard for my dreams.\

Inner Me

You are a warrior
You need not let others fool you
I know that you might have felt completely lost sometimes
But remember one thing always that you are the only saviour for yourself
Be a person full of passion not a person full of love
I have seen people falling in love but i have never seen people rising in love
I can tell you this by my own experience
For me true love was my friends , my second family
There was a time i needed my friends the most but that was the only time i realised that one day everybody is going to betray you
So never ever give the key to your happiness in somebody else's hands
My bad times have showed me so many real faces and then i was left with few but true friends
There was a time when i hated myself
But this is life and it goes on and that is what i did , i moved on
So now with so many changes , i am the only reason that leads to my happiness
Nobody can destroy me now
My self-respect is my top most priority
No friend but my family has always supported me in being strong
Always remember one thing-

Quantity of people in a group doesn't matters
Quality of people matters

So here are few lines by me -

ज़िन्दगी तुझे चलना सिखाएगी,

तू कदम बढ़ा के तो देख।

ज़िन्दगी तुझे जीना सिखायेगी

तू बाहें खोल के तो देख।

अपनो की भीड़ में,

मैंने खुद को अकेला पाया है।

मगर शाम ढलते,

मैंने खुद को ही अपना पाया है।

Gaurav Nautiyal

Gaurav Nautiyal is 20 years old and he belongs from Dehradun.He is pursuing Bachelor of Arts from SGRR college, Dehradun.He is also doing diploma in Engineering. He comes from a family of 5 where he is the youngest one.His idea of achieving success is to achieve greater heights in life and make his parents very proud.Gaurav is a person with strong mindset and is introvert by nature.He loves to write in his leisure time.He also loves to explore new places and is a travel freak.Gaurav's company is best.He knows how to make somebody smile in their toughest times and ends up doing the same.His free advice to everyone is that life is like a puzzle and you have to keep solving it until it becomes clear.

Gaurav Nautiyal can be contacted at his IG handle which is @_gaurav_nautiyal\

Lost Emotions

My overthinking is something you hate the most ;
Still chin on hand , thinking when you will be mine
?
In our love show , you are the judge and I am your
host ;
You know I want to be with you all my time .
Shall I compare you to a cup of tea ?
You are like a crown of beauty and all its pride ;
Darling love is like a substance from honey bee ;
Oh ! No how can I forget, when first your eye I
eye'd .
But NO ! The love I got is never I thought ;
Your love is not love , stop , look through my eye;
With your yes , my dreams, my goals ,my needs, is
all lost ;
Many times I explain many times I cry .
Therefore I hide and smile when you are with me ,
And our fights by choice we flattered to be .

I Hide

I just can't explain how it feel ;
So I stitch my lips to low down my louder scream .
So young , still trying , smiling in the mirror ;
Only learn, how to make fake laugh clear .
The smile on my face is a forever sin ;
My line b/w happy and sad is very thin .
Now i am so used to it , living without no tears ;
Because it's been this way from many years .
One day my MAHADEV will make my soul fully heal ;
I just can't explain how it feel .

Tanya Rai

This is tanya rai , a student from gorakhpur.I dream to become artist, and writer. My hobby is to play guitar, reading books, and sketching. I am quite friendly with everyone. My instagram handle is @tanya_rai______ you can follow me here
Thankyou.

I Failed My Way To Success

Someone who fails is, someone who has challenged himself

the Black day; 18th march 2018'. I was lying on my bed and thinking about my past, and it was exactly-'03:00AM'.

It's common to think about our past, but many of us don't care about it or take it easily, and move on in life....

Yeah!! It's a great thing to ignore or avoid and moving on in life, but really it's not easy to forget it...

'Yes you and me' are similar who think about our past, but it depend on what type of past is it. Some of us had their lovely, sad, happy, funny broken, darkest, depressed neither painful past.

'People say's that our past doesn't effect on us and our future'.but it's wrong, it effects, on our life and on those life who think reassemble like me, (my past). It's relatable to my school days.

It always broke my strength when I start thinking about it at '03:00AM'.

'Failure' is a word which hurts to everyone. Everyone fails once in their life, and move towards the future with positive thoughts. But I'm different , many people said me that have positive thought and move on in life that will never effect on you.

'But no sometime we think that we can't..... '

We set it that ' we can't' think good because we didn't give our best that time and our soul knows that..... That's why we easily give up. Our heart know what we want, we need, & we feel, but our mind doesn't. You know why? Because our mind is that thing which we make once remind about something will always make us remember that we have this thought, this work, at this time - like this my mind also make me always remind that I'm 'failure' and useless, I can't do anything in my life. This makes me and my soul scream out at '03:00 Am' thoughts.

'Failure is a key to success'

So, I also never give up and I tried lot-a-lot but now I'm on my way of life. But still those thoughts irritate me at night '03:00AM'

I cried out silently and my pain also flow with my cried soul.

Speak the truth even if your voice shakes face the failure even if your soul breaks.

Saloni Gupta

Saloni Gupta is 19 years old and hails from Uttrakhand.She belongs to a nuclear family of 3 where she is the youngest.She is a budding writer and a poet too.Saloni is pursuing her studies from Shreeja College, Dehradun. She is also a Co-Author of the book 'Indie Violet'.She is extroverted by nature and is very friendly.She wants to achieve success as a General ranked officer in an Indian Army field.Her goal is to make her parents proud and put smile on everybody's face.She always tells people to stay strong and smile in every obstacles in life.For Saloni, her mother is an Idol inspiration of hard work and never giving up in life.

Hobbies: Writing, Gardening, Cooking, Baking, Singing.

Saloni believes that words are very powerful and lasts forever.For her, words are an immense way of portraying thoughts and emotions.

Heavy Heart

I kept those emotions within me,
Too tired to portray them to somebody of me.
Isn't it hard to stay calm,
I questioned why should I fake my charm.
I have been graving so much inside me,
Just hiding every pain that's digged deep inside me.
Sometime its tough to control those tears,
Therefore,
I just sit and ask how this pain I will even bear.
This heart is craving for a shoulder to cry and lean on,
But Somewhere ,
I know there's a warrior inside me that will certainly won.
A heart is too heavy to lift it up,
I wish
I could rest and now give up.
A heart is too heavy to hold back those emotions,
I wish
I could scream and unload every portion.
I wish,
I could unload every portion!

फौजी

आज गर्व से घर लौटा हूँ, इस धरा पर
मैं शहीद हो आया हूँ।
जानता हूँ, रो रही होगी मेरी माँ...
गले से लिपटकर,
बुला रही होगी मेरी माँ।
शायद, आज पिता के कंधे मैं उच्चे कर दू।
वो गर्व से खड़े हो,
और उनका नाम मैं आज कर दू।
ये खाकी वर्दी है जो मेरी,
इसे तू संभाल कर रखना।
ये यादें है जो मेरी,
इसे तू समेट कर रखना।
मैं आज गर्व से सो रहा हूँ,
इस सफर को,
अब अलविदा मैं कह रहा हूँ।
सीने पर फूल लिए,
अब मुस्कुरा रहा हूँ मैं।
इस ताबूत मे बंद हुए,
अब जा रहा हूँ मैं।
अब इस देश को,

एक वीर और मिल गया।
उस कायर दुश्मन को,
यूँ खौफ में दे गया।
एक फौजी हूँ,
जो ना झुकेगा, ना डरेगा!
सीना चौड़ा कर,
यूँ गर्व से रहेगा!

MOHIT MISHRA

This is Mohit Mishra.
I am from Lucknow, Uttar Pradesh.
My hobbies are writing, singing, painting and acting.
You can find my writeups on my Instagram account @the.writers.era
By profession I am a student.
Thank you.

स्कूल

वो सर्द हवा अब कहा मिलेगी,
वो गर्म जोश अब ठंडा पड़ जाएगा,
कहा पता था की अब स्कूल का ये
सुहाना सफर एक पल आते ही थम जाएगा।
ना होश रह्ता था की क्या कर रहे है,
और ना ही होश मे आना चाहते थे।
ह्तो बस कुछ खुशियों के पल,
अपनी यादों मे बसाना चाहते थे।
जब याद आएंगे ये पल तो बस अफसोस,
रह जाएगा की काश ये पल कभी ना खतम होते,
और वो स्कूल हमारा, और हम बस उस स्कूल के ही होते।
वो दोस्त भी याद आएंगे, वो उनका प्यार भी याद आएगा,
वो उनका हसना भी याद आएगा, और हसाना भी याद
आएगा,
वो उनका रोना भी याद आएगा, और शायद उनका आज
का रुलाना कल चेहरे पर एक मीठी सी मुस्कान दे
जाएगा।
अब कहाँ वो teachers की आवाज़ आएगी की 'hands
at the back' or 'be in a decorum' आवाज़ तो बस

दिल से आएगी की we are never gonna forget you my second dad and mum.

Shayari

टूटे सितारे की तू क्या आरज़ू करता है,
टूटे हुए ख्वाबो की तू क्या इस ज़माने
के सामने नुमाईश करता है,
ज़रा अपना जज़्बा तो दिखा इस दुनिया को,
फिर देखना कैसे ये ज़माना तुझे अपना बनाने की ख्वाईश
करता है।

कुछ वो भी सोचते,
कुछ हम्भी खयाल करते,
फिर आँखों ही आँखों मे,
हाल-ए-दिल बयां करते,
मगर उन्हे कहा थी हमसे मिलने की फुर्सत,
नही तो हम्भी उनसे उनकी बेरुखी का सवाल करते।

Being lonely from inside,
And friendly from outside,
Being not able to express the griefs and sorrows you
are suffering from,
Knowing that your heart is haunting and sobing
ruthlessly inside you,
But at last you have to remain strong in front of the
world.
These are some of the toughest situations faced by
every teenager.

Dhivya Rajamani

I am Dhivya Rajamani working in Bangalore at NTT DATA. I love to travel to new places and meet new friends to hear their stories. I often write thoughts that rely on expressing myself or the wounds of others.Instagram – thecoffee_writer.

Your Own Path!!!

That was the moment I decided,
I want to fly from everything, the drama from my family and the society evil talks.

It was almost a year I expended. After my graduation, I stood up for a year to fight what I want to continue. But my parents conclude in getting a decent job which is also respectable for society. Every single day in a year was meaningless to me, fighting, twisting and turning on the bed, sleepless nights, overthinking beyond the limit, the fluctuation between choosing the career I love or career I try by parents wishes.

Thoughts arose in me, why is this world prevailing when I can not even decide the career, cannot marry the girl I love, not worthy to talk what I think is valid and million number of questions whirling around my mind.

Watching the movies that ended up happily, reading the stories proposing a positive ending, the life of me cannot be positive unless I made it. So, I decided to step out of my house to pursue my wish and live life on my own independently.

Achieving on the path you choose make parents appreciate one day. If it's not now, then never I can choose my career I deserve, the identity of my future. In Life, it is important to fly beyond failures and hurt, and I decided to fly high.

Shreya Gupta

I am Shreya Gupta from Basti, Uttarpradesh
I love hindi language and writing is my soul's deepest passion . I want my parents to be proud of my work.

ज़िन्दगी

चलो ज़िन्दगी जीने की हम वजह ढूंढते है,
खुशियों से जगमगाता एक शहर ढूंढते है,
छूटा संग कितनो का इस भाग दौड़ भरी जिंदगी में,
चलो उन रिश्तों की आज हम गिरह ढूंढते है।

चलो खुलकर जिए हर एक लम्हे को,
ऐसी मस्ती करने वाली हम जगह ढूंढते है,
गुज़ारे है हमने भी कई वक़्त अंधेरो में,
चलो आज उन अंधेरो की हम नई सुबह ढूंढते है।

उलझी हुई सी पहेली है ये ज़िन्दगी,
चलो हम उन्हें सुलझाने की कोशिश करते है,
अपने देश की उन्नती और विकाश के लिए,
आओ हम सभी जन एक होकर चलते है।

कभी न छोड़े सच की राहे,
आओ ऐसी सीख हम सबको देते है,
इंसानियत जिंदा रहे हम सभी के दिलो में,
आओ हम मिलकर यही दुआ करते है ।

कुछ बातें

कुछ बातें है अनकही सी,
जो आज तुमको बतानी है,
प्यार हो गया है मुझे तुमसे,
पर मैने भी ये बात अब जानी है।

जानता हूँ तुम किसी और की हो,
पर खुद को ये बात नही समझानी है,
दूर से ही देख लेता हू तुम्हे तो,
दिल को मेरे राहत मिल जाती हैं।

बहुत दर्द होता है तुम्हे किसी और के साथ देखकर,
पर खुशी तुम्हारी उससे है , अब मैने ये बात मानी है,
दोस्त ही बनकर सही,तुम्हे खुशिया दे सकू,
बस यही तमन्ना मेरी ज़िंदगानी है।

जहा भी रहो खुश रहो तुम,
मैने ये दुआ अपने रब से मांगी है ,
कभी मुश्किल में पड़ना तो याद करना मुझे,
ये दोस्त तुम्हारी खिदमत में सदा हाज़िर है।

Ayushi Kamble

This is ayushi kamble. I'm 18 years old my hometown is Yavatmal, Maharashtra. I like reading books, solitude, the nature, History, Philosphy, Politics and searching about various different subjects. I have fond interest in writing since early childhood. But only thought of becoming a writer a couple of years ago when I wrote for my School magazine. If you're interested in reading my thoughts you are most welcomed at my Instagram page.
@ayushiikamble.

The Sacred Thread Of Love

What is Love? I bet many broken hearts out there have the answer to this. And many young hearts in love, are pondering upon it. So what really is love? Is it Emotive? Or is it sacrificial? Painful? Physical? Or Spiritual?

The answer- All of it. Love is emotive, sacrificial, painful, physical and spiritual. Love is a lot of things combined, it is not just one thing.

Now what is it to live? Is it to breathe? To overcome obstacles? To fulfil our dreams? Or to love?

The answer- It's all of these things, combined! A lot of people love and forget to live, and a lot of people live and forget to love.

The most important thing to live is love, we can only survive in this cruel world. If we have love, and are being loved. I've heard a lot of people say that there's an invisible thread connecting all of us, and everything around us. And I firmly believe, it's a thread soaked in love. A thread connecting our hearts and bringing them together.

A thread that the souls follow when looking for their one true mate.

And I believe this thread has a lot of stories to tell.

Stories of loyalty and betrayal. Stories from the very first time a man fell in love. And stories of tragic endings.

For love is eternal, and we are mere objects.

Love is contentment and we are the container.

Love is the mist covering the mountains and we are the cool dew drops left behind.

Our one true purpose in this world is to love each other. To be kind with each other. And to support each other. Selflessly. Completely.

Love is Meera loving Krishna with all her heart.

Love is Muhammad choosing to be a humble slave than a king.

Love is Qays declaring himself Majnun Layla.

Love is Rani Laxmi Bai fighting the enemies till her last breathe for her nation.

And Love is the universe. And the thread encircling it.

Damini Upadhyay

Born on 28th of September in Rajasthan she grew up in Gujarat. Currently pursuing Master's in literature, she is in love with writing and exploring the different forms of it. She believes, "When nobody listens, your diary/notepad does".

You can savour her poetic side on her Instagram page @think_aloud_00 where she is growing her passion into something exquisite.

The Heaven And Hell Of Love

.

The thought of love itself
Is heaven for some
While hell for others
Nobody knows what it is
Even the ones who feel it
They too sometimes get stuck
With a question in their heads
Is it love?
Sometimes it seems the beautiful feeling ever
And sometimes to never feel it ever
Its a roller coaster ride
Having both of its sides
Love is not just a thing
It's millions of little things
Some pretty some ugly
But no one would regret it definitely.

Life Goes On

You go through hundreds of pain
Each of which stays in the heart as stain
And all of the tough strain
Just keeps on adding in the brain
But the brain and heart takes it all
Whether it's huge or small
Cause they know its life
And it comes with a lot of strife
We go through it and we learn
Growth and peace we earn
It's upon the person totally
Either to stuck or move peacefully
This is life and it works that way
Either to lose and quit
Or to learn and win to move away
Cause it's life and it goes on!

Sakshi Agrawal

She is SAKSHI AGRAWAL, daughter of MR. Gopal Agrawal. She is from muzaffarpur, bihar. She is just 18 year old, A little realistic, A lot poetic. She is just in the way to make her father feel proud. She is a great dreamer, just try to pen down whatever comes in her heart. She says writing is her soul's deepest passion. You can contact her via instagram @pen._vibes.

Sorry

Sorry!
For my sweet melodious voice Which allows you to raise your noise
For my innocent eyes Now everything is so changed
Which peep out for your bloody lies
You and are no more same

Sorry!
Because you don't deserve the love I built up so long for you
My believe, my trust
All turn you to be the worst
gave you my throne
Where all the misunderstandings grew

Sorry!
I Gave you the chance To break my heart which lasted long
All the promises made to me Gave me more wounds to heal
All the plans of our future Turned out to be the dilly dally with suture

Sorry!
And thank you too!
To teach me that forever is a lie
Everything lies between hello and goodbye Waiting for you
Is gonna hurt me more
But now I will laugh at your foul
Because leaving me is gonna be the reason of houl.

Chirag L Sagar

Chirag L Sagar is a 1st year MBBS student studying at Srinivas Institute of Medical Sciences and Research Centre,Mangalore. His hobbies are poetry, reading - books,novels, autobiographies,philately, listening to songs,sports like cricket and badminton,cooking. He is a medico by profession and a writer by passion. His best friend Nihar,has always been his inspiration and motivation to do great in whatever he does. His dream is to become an Oncologist and a successful writer.
Instagram : @chirag_cls18 Facebook : Chirag LSagar.

Dear Love

To the sweetest person I know,
To the one with gleaming eyes and dazzling looks,
With a serene smile,
Which makes my day.
To the person with a golden heart
and burning passion for life.
Your love is the only thing I need,
And your smile is the medicine
for my illness.
I dream of none,
Except you.
Please stay besides me,
For all the good and bad times
We will tackle together,
I would love to hold you hand,
Forever, till my last breath.

I know,
I'm not the person you wished of,
And dreamt for.
I may not be your perfect partner in all ways.
But,
I'll always try my best,
To keep you happy and
see your cute innocent smile,
See you happy all the time,
Give all the hugs and cuddles you want,
Shower truck loads of love and affection.

And I promise,
That there will be not even a single day,
Of seeing tears in your eyes.
Last but not the least,
This is a promise,
For a lifetime.

What Is Life ?

Life is a cycle of birth and death.
Nevertheless comparable to two sides of a coin.
Imagine everything surrounding you starts dying,
And don't realize your next step.
Remember that your life is beautiful,
And as a phase of life,
The wheel of destiny changes it's side.
Life is always uncertain,
You never know your next step.
Life always changes it's direction,
From winter to spring to autumn to fall,
It's always precious.
Life can be cruel at times,
The winter in your life takes you away with it,
And spring follows it.
That's the rule of nature,
What dies has to be replenished.
Life is beautiful,
And live your life to the fullest.

Sejal Rawat

Sejal Rawat, an exuberant 18 years old poet/ painter/ artist who loves to paint the world through her imagination was born in New Delhi. Originally from Uttarakhand. She is currently pursuing Journalism and Mass Communication from Lingays Lalita Devi Institute Of Management and Science, Chattarpur, New Delhi. She mostly writes about moon.This is her 2nd poem which has been published. To know more about her you can follow her on mirakee and mail her at sejalrawat.sr@gmail.com.

चांद नज़र आया

देखो आज फिर ज़मीन पे चांद नज़र आया है।
कुछ इस तरह अपनी रोशनी फैलागाया कि बाकि सब नज़र अंदाज़ करवागया।
तेरी तारीफ में अब क्या लिखूं मै बस इतना जानती हूं कि जब वो चांद इतराता है तो मैं उसे तेरी तस्वीर दिखाकर चुप कर्वदिती हूं।
मैं तो तेरे रूप को देखकर मदहोश हो चुकी हूं।
शायद अब अगले बरस ही होश आये।
हे चांद!! तुझसे है ये की फरहात बक्ष अगले बरस फिर आना अपना ये नूरानी चेहरा दिखाने।

यादों की दुनिया

हमने तो सुना था कि बहुत खुबसूरत होति है ये यादों की
दुनिया,
फिर जब आज़ मैंने अपनी किताब के कुछ पन्ने पलट के
देखे तो वो यादें क्यों गुलाब के फूलों मे लगे कांटो सी चुबी|
क्यों मैं मुरझाये हुऐ गुलाब के बिखरते हुए पंखुड़ीयो की
तरह बिखरने लगी ...
सहि कहा था किसिने कि हमारे बीते हुऐ कल के छोटे -
छोटे तुकडे हमारी यादों मे मुहफुज रहते है ...
तभी तो देखो,
ना सिर्फ तूम्हारी यादें बलकि तुम्हारा दिया हुआ गुलाब
आज भी
मेरे दिल की किताब मे कितना मेहफुज है।

Subhransu Padhy

Hey Readers,
This is Subhransu Padhy . He Comes Form a Small Town Of Odisha . He is a Student , Poet And Coauthor Of 100+ Anthologies . He Has Earned 450+ Rewards From Various Literary Clubs Till Now. He Mostly Writes On Social Issues and Wants To Change The Society With His Words . Got a Very Creative Mind Which Helps Him To Pendown All His Feelings In His Writings . Loves To Present The Social Issues In a Very Sarcastical Manner . But His Writings On Love Are Really Exceptional . Hope You All Will Enjoy His Works . He Feels Very Great To Be The Part Of This Masterpiece " 3 A.M. THOUGHTS

एक और कोशिश

सौ बार गिरने के बावजूद भी एक बार
फिर उठने की कोशिश कर सकता हूँ,
हार को सफलता का सीढ़ी मानकर
फिर मंजिल के लिए बढ़ सकता हूँ,
हाँ मुझे खुद पर इतना भरोसा है कि
मैं एक और कोशिश कर सकता हूँ।
लक्ष्य प्राप्ति के लिए मैं
दिन रात एक कर सकता हूँ,
मेरे परिश्रम के सामने हालातों को
झुकने पर मजबूर कर सकता हूँ,
हाँ मुझे खुद पर इतना भरोसा है कि
मैं एक और कोशिश कर सकता हूँ।
मैं विगत के दुःख कष्ट को भूलकर
फिर से मंजिल की ओर बढ़ सकता हूँ,
हर मुश्किलों का करने के लिए सामना खुद
को उतना काबिल और मजबूत बना सकता हूँ,
हाँ मुझे खुद पर इतना भरोसा है कि
मैं एक और कोशिश कर सकता हूँ।
हज़ारों बाधाओं के बाबजूद भी मैं सफलता
के शिखर तक पहुँच सकता हूँ,
चाहे फूल हो या काँटा हर परिस्थिति
को पार कर मैं निखर सकता हूँ,
हाँ मुझे खुद पर इतना भरोसा है कि
मैं एक और कोशिश कर सकता हूँ।

<u>प्यार का नशा</u>

इंसान कब इस मधुर नशे के दबोच
में आ जाए उसे खुद भी पता नहीं होता,
वरना १७ हज़ार गोपियाँ जिसके पीछे थे
वह कृष्णा एक राधा के लिए नहीं रोता।

प्यार तो प्यार होता है साहब इसमें
जाती-धर्म , उंच-नीच का कोई भेदभाव नहीं होता,
वरना सारी दुनिया को जीतने वाला नेपोलियन
मामूली जोसफिन के पीछे पागल नहीं होता।

अगर जानना है इसका नशा तो किसी
प्रेमी जोड़ी से जाकर पूछो एक बार,
लिखकर देता हूँ जनाब जवाब तो एक ही मिलेगा
उनके प्रियतमा के आँखों से बढ़कर कोई और नशा नहीं
होता।

Jeevika Phagwani

This is Jeevika Phagwani, a college student. I am 19 years old. I really like to dance, and sing as well. I have many friends back from school and we have had alot of fun for so many years. And it's been a hell of a journey, all the ups and downs, there were friends who were there for me and i was there for some. This is it.

ऐ ज़िन्दगी

ऐ ज़िन्दगी,
मैं आज बहुत खुश हूँ और अब लगता है तुम भी अच्छी हो, चीज़े समझ से जो आने लगी है। आज 19 साल हो गए हमे साथ चलते हुए तुमने ना जाने क्या क्या सीखा है, कुछ चीज़ें बर्दाश्त के परे थे, कुछ की अहमियत तुमने बहुत खूबी सीखी है। मोह्हबत तो देखी थी छोटी उम्र में उसको समझने का सफर बहुत लम्बा था, बहुत लोग आए कुछ रुके कुछ बिन देखे चले गए । बस एक तुम थी जिसने साथ निभाया । अगर देखू उस 13 साल की बच्ची को जो ज़माने में बहकी थी, यारो की गिरफ्त में आसमान तोड़ बैठी थी तो सब नादान सा लगता है। अब ना वो दोस्त मौजूद है ना वो लड़की ज़िंदा है , है तो कुछ यादें।उस वक़्त कमियां जो खलती थी , दो नम्बर काम आने पर वो बेइज़्ज़ती से लगती थी अब ना उन नम्बरो का महत्व है ना उन यादों में जाने की चाहत । ज़िन्दगी तू ले आई अब जो दूर है , देखा कौन भला कौन राम-दूत है। खुशी की चाहत तो बचपन से थी बस अनजान थी टी इससे की उसकी बनायत मुझसे ही थी। उसकी खोज में ना जाने कितनों का दिल दुखाया है , ज़िन्दगी तुमने बहुत कुछ सिखाया है।कोसा तो तुम्हे बहुत है पर वक़्त पर तुमने ही साथ निभाया है।अब शिकवे नही बीते कल से मुजे उसने ही आज मुझे बनाया है। शुक्रिया कहु तो कम ज़िन्दगी तूने ही आज मुझे इस मकाम तक पहुँचाया है।

Alankar Sandeep Maeenkar

Hello my name is Alankar sandeep maeenkar
age 24 from mumbai
I am a professional footballer with 4 world records
and also an aircraft engineering student .
Instagram- smartyfreestyle

६ साल

हम देखते रहे आँखों में उनकी और वक़्त वहीं ठेहर गया,
बस बन गया एक रिश्ता ऐसा जो प्यार में उलझकर रेह गया.

तुम साथ थी तो लगता था जैसे हा मुझमें भी कोई बात थी,
क्यूंकि एक आप थी जो सही गलत हर वक़्त मेरे साथ थी.

वो दिन वो रातें वो तुमसे की हुई सारी मुलाकातें,
तुम्हारे साथ गुजारे हर पल आंखों में बारिश बनकर थे आते.

हालात से मजबुर इतने की कुछ कर नहीं सकते थे,
तुम्हारे बिन जीना क्या मर भी नहीं सकते थे,
सिर्फ वो सांसें ज़िंदा रेह गई थी मुझमें बाकी,
जान तो वैसे भी आप जाते जाते ले ही चुके थे।

 मगर वो नशा कुछ और ही था रोज जीने रोज़ मरने में,
 वो मज़ा कुछ और ही था तुम्हे फिर याद करने में,
बोहोत धुंडा तुम्हे ज़िन्दगी के सारे पन्नों पे,
पर था वो वक़्त का साथ नसीबों को हमारे उस बिछड़ने मे।

हां देने को सहारे हमें वैसे तो मिलते थे सब,
पर मिला ना सहारा जिनका चाहिए था तब,
पत्थर था सीना हमने भी खूब आजमाया,
जो दर्द बीता दिल पर वो बस जानता था रब।

किस्मत का हाथ नहीं था सर पे उसने भी ऐसा खेल खेला,
जैसे तारों में है चांद वैसे हमें कर दिया भीड़ में अकेला,

कैसे करता बयां तुम्हे हालत इस दिल की,
कोई झेल नहीं पाएगा कसम से जो मेने था झेला।
गुजरे ६ साल कुछ ऐसे आज खुदा ने हमें फिर से मिलाया है,
वीरान ज़िन्दगी को आज हमारे जीना फिर से सिखाया है,
ताकत तो प्यार में थी मेरे और वो किए इंतज़ार में,
जो कभी सोचा नहीं था वो हासिल करके दिखाया है।

Bhumika Katyal

This is Bhumika Katyal from Agra,
I am pursing B.B.A and want to be a bussiness woman in future , writing is my passion , I write with my heart out , using easy and contemporary form of language so, every lay person can understand and enjoy the same .
Instagram id :
@alfaazo_se_pehchan

जब बात एक लड़की की हो

कभी समझ नहीं आई यह रीति ;जब बात एक लड़की की हो तो ही क्यों सवाल ही सवाल सबको याद आते हैं क्यों उसके अपने भी उसे अजनबी बन जाते है; उसे समझ नहीं पाते है।

क्यों सब यह भूल जाते हैं वो भी एक इंसान है उसे भी जीने का उतना ही हक है;जितना सबको है; उसे भी अपने हिसाब से चलने का हक है ;जैसे दूसरों को, क्यों वो रिश्तो के नाम पर इंसानियत भी भूल जाते हैं।

यह क्योंकि रीति उसके सपनों को चूर- चूर कर जाती है ? एक लड़की से उससे लड़की क्यों बनाया यह सवाल कर जाती है।

दिल से चूर-चूर होकर भी वो सबके सामने खुश होने का दिखावा करना नहीं भूलती है;तब भी जब बात एक लड़की की हो
तब ही कायदे -कानून, जंजीरे सबको क्यों याद आती है, तब
ही क्यों सही गलत सबको समझ आता है, क्यों नापा जाता है उसे तराजू की तरह क्यों उसे समझने की बारी पर सब बेदिल हो जाते हैं।

क्यों जब बात एक लड़की की हो तो रिवाजों की दुनिया में उसे कैद कर लिया जाता है, उससे अपने लिए ही जीने से गैर कर दिया जाता है।

<u>लकीरें</u>

लकीरों में क्या है हां,यह तो नहीं जानते हम; मगर फासलों को तय ना कर पाएं इतने भी बेगैर नहीं हैं हम|

हां,माना अपने हिसाब से तय नहीं कर सकते, यह सफर पर हां इतने भी कमजोर नहीं हैं,हम की ढल जाए इन लकीरों के हवाले...

हां मालूम है गिरेंगे मगर कोई नहीं उठ कर फिर चल देंगे एक सकून सी सांस भर लेंगे की हां माना यह लकीरे हवाले नहीं हमारे पर तब भी झुके नहीं हम इन लकीरों के आगे।

GAUTAM AGARWAL

I am Gautam Agarwal
Basically A freelancer And a BDA In testbook .
Travel freak.
Lives in city bahraich.

प्यार

प्यार सिर्फ एक शब्द नही,एक एहसास है, कीमत जानते है वो लोग जिनके पास है।

मुरजाये हुए चेहरे पे जो मुस्कुराहट ले आये ये प्यार शब्द इतना खास होता है।

महबूब सच्चा हो तो ज़िन्दगी आसान सी लगती है थोड़ा सा रूठ जाए तो परेशान सी लगती है।

हर एक को समझ आ जाए ये इतना भी आसान नही जो करता है जी ते जी हज़ार बार मरता है ये जो लोग बताते है ये इसकी पहचान नही।

कृष्णा ने प्यार का पैगाम कुछ इस कदर दिया है राधा से प्यार अधूरा किया है।

प्यार का मकसद किसी को पाना नही है अगर ऐसा सोचते हो तो तुमने अभी प्यार के बारे में जाना नही है।

एक रिश्ते को प्यारा सा नाम दे जाता है प्यार कुछ इस कदर अपना पैगाम दे जाता है।

SUGANDHA VERMA

मेरा नाम सुगंधा वर्मा है और मैं बर्डपुर , जिला सिद्धार्थ नगर की निवासी हूँ। मुझे लोगों को खुशी देना अच्छा लगता है गेम खेलना पसंद है घूमना पसंद है नई नई तरह की कपड़े पहनना पसंद है।

जिंदगी और प्यार

जिंदगी बहुत ही खूबसूरत है जिंदगी हमें बहुत कुछ सिखाती है कौन अपने हैं कौन पराई हैं जिसको जिंदगी जीना आ गया तो समझिए उसे सब कुछ आ गया पर इतना आसान भी नहीं है जिंदगी को जीना में बहुत कुछ खोना पड़ता है बहुत रोना पड़ता है बहुत सारे संकट आते हैं पर जिसने इसे हर तरीके से अपनी जिंदगी को पार कर लिया उस इंसान को जिंदगी खूबसूरत लगती है पता है जिंदगी बहुत प्यारी होती है बहुत ही कम लोगों को इतनी अच्छी जिंदगी नसीब में मिलती है पर सही मायने में जिंदगी लोग अपने लिए नहीं अपनों के लिए जीते हैं जिसको कहते हैं हम परिवार पता है परिवा की खुशी के लिए किसी भी हद तक जाकर मनुष्य उस खुशी को पूरा कर सकता है सच कहूं तो मनुष्य परिवार के बारे में सोच कर अपनी खुशी को त्याग देते हैं क्या अच्छा लगता है क्या नहीं उन्हें क्या करना पसंद है अपनी सारी खुशियां परिवार के लिए लोग छोड़ देते हैं कि लोग क्या कहेंगे मेरा परिवार क्या सोचने लगेगा मतलब खुद की जिंदगी दूसरों पर छोड़ देते हैं की लोग क्या कहेंगे पर यह गलत है अपनी खुशी को पूरी करनी चाहिए खुल के जीना चाहिए क्योंकि लोग क्या कहेंगे यह भूल जाइए आप गलत रहोगे तो भी बोलेंगे सही रहोगे तो भी बोलेंगे क्योंकि दूसरे लोग कभी आपको खुश नहीं देखना चाहेंगे तकलीफ में रहोगे आप तो भी कहेंगे उसको कितनी तकलीफ है बार-बार

कहेंगे और खुश रहोगे तो भी कहेंगे कितना खुश है कितना खुश है किसी भी तरीके से जीने नहीं देंगे आपको इसलिए दूसरों के बारे में ना सोच कर अपने बारे में सोचिए कि आपको अपनी जिंदगी कैसे जीनी है !पता है ? ज्यादातर लोग अंधविश्वास पर जीते हैं !भगवान की मूर्ति को पूजते हैं कि भगवान है !यह जो चीज दरअसल इस दुनिया में है !ही नहीं अपने अंदर है मन में अपने विश्वास में है!आप खुद पर विश्वास रखेंगे यह चीज है! तो है वह आपके मानने के ऊपर है पर लोग ऐसा नहीं करते हैं! अंधविश्वास पर ज्यादा भरोसा करते हैं !जैसे मूर्तियों की पूजा करना. फूल चढ़ाते हैं बहुत तरह के जेवर पहनाते हैं !साड़ी पहनाते हैं! मूर्ति की पूजा करते हैं! जिसमें जान है ही नहीं अगर लोग वही चीज एक गरीब इंसान को दे तो उसके बदले में कई लाख गुना ज्यादा आपको वापस मिलेगा जो खुशियां गरीब को दे सकते हैं ना वह दीजिए फिर देखिए कितनी खुशी मिलती है उनको खुश देख कर पता है मैं अपनी जिंदगी इस तरीके से जीना चाहती हूं ? कि मेरे जिंदगी के हिस्से की सारी खुशियां गरीबों के साथ मनाऊं की मेरे पास इतने पैसे हो की धरती पर जितनी भी गरीब है उन सभी को अपने जैसा एक समान बना सकूं कभी वह किसी के सामने भीख ना मांगे मुझे बहुत दया आती है जब किसी बुजुर्ग को बच्चों को भीख मांगते हैं सड़क पर मुझे बहुत तकलीफ होती है किसी भी तरीके से अपने घर को चलाने के लिए वह इतना त्याग करते हैं मुझे बहुत ज्यादा बुरा लगता है और मैं भगवान से हमेशा कहती हूं! भगवान सबको एक जैसा बनाऊं मेरी बस यही

प्रार्थना रहती है !भगवान से एक जैसे सब लोग एक साथ रहे सभी लोगों के दिल में एक दूसरे के लिए प्यार हो अगर वह अपने हैं तो भी नहीं है तो भी प्यार हो सब लोग अगर ऐसे हो जाते तो कभी इस धरती पर कोई मरने के लिए भगवान से प्रार्थना नहीं करेगा क्योंकि यहीं पर स्वर्ग है बस हमारी सोच पर यह बनता है कि हमें दूसरों के साथ वैसे ही पेश आना है जैसे हम अपनों के सामने आते हैं मानते हैं प्यार करते हैं इज्जत देते हैं सम्मान देते हैं! वैसे ही हम लोगों को देंगे ना तो बदले में भी हमें भी मिलेगा और जिंदगी को जीने में बहुत मजा आएगा सच कहूं तो लोग स्वर्ग और नर्क ऊपर खोजते हैं !और सही मायने में इस धरती पर ही है! बस अपनी अंदर उसको खोजना पड़ेगा कि किस चीज को आप करके इस धरती पर रहकर स्वर्ग बना सकते हो ?और किस चीज पर ना करके नर्क बना सकते हो

आपकी प्यारी दोस्त
सुगंधा वर्मा

Yash Soni

Name: Yash Soni
Insta- shinsoniyash
Profession: Actor, Singer, Writer, Lyricist, Music
Producer, & passion follower

मुझे जवाब पता है

रास्ते और मंज़िल एक है,
तेरे सवाल अनेक है,
तेरे भरोसे का,
मुझे जवाब पता है ।

अगर में तुमसे पुछू,
की तू मुझे कितना चाहती है,
और क्या मुझपे भरोसा करती है,
मुझे जवाब पता है ।

ये अतरंगी दुनिया है,
यहां बेहतरीन कलाकार है,
तेरे कलाकारी सवालों का,
मुझे जवाब पता है।

मौत को देखा हूँ,
अकेला भी रहता हूँ,
तेरे ज़िन्दगी को लेकर जो सवाल है,
उनका, मुझे जवाब पता है।

तेरे दुख, तेरे सुख, तेरी हसी, तेरी खुशी,
तेरी चाहत, तेरी जरूरत, तेरा ख्वाब, तेरा हक़ीक़त,
तेरे हर सवाल का,

मुझे जवाब पता है।

पर में अगर तुमसे कोई सवाल करूं,
कुछ पूछूँ मुझे लेकर,
क्या तुम जवाब दे पाओगी,
उसका भी मुझे जवाब पता है।

प्यार मोहब्बत इंसान को बेबस बनाता है,
यही तोह तुम्हारा कहना है,
तुमसे मैंने जब पूछा तुमने ऐसा क्यों बोला,
 उस सवाल का भी मुझे जवाब पता है।

तेरे कहने से पहले,
मुझे जवाब पता है,
और तेरे सोचने के बाद,
मुझे जवाब पता है।

हाँ मुझे जवाब पता है,
मुझे जवाब पता है।